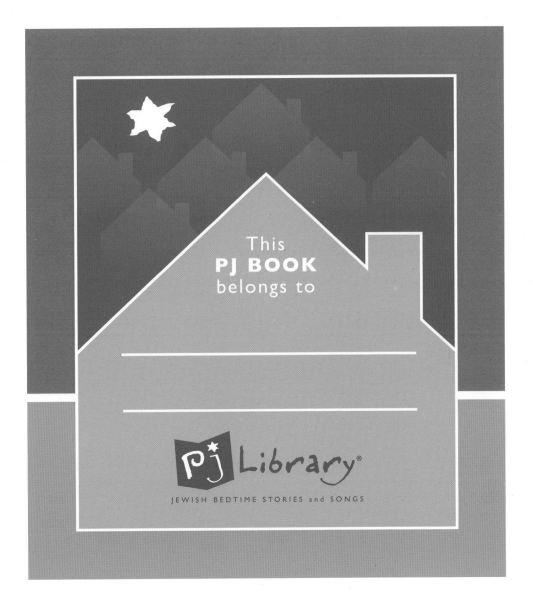

This
PJ BOOK
belongs to

PJ Library®

JEWISH BEDTIME STORIES and SONGS

For Jasper, who is a force of nature
—L.S.

For Cosmo and Misha
—J.I.

Text copyright © 2012 by Laurel Snyder
Cover art and interior illustrations copyright © 2012 by Jui Ishida

All rights reserved.
Published in the United States by Random House Children's Books, a division of Penguin Random House LLC, New York.

Random House and the colophon are registered trademarks of Penguin Random House LLC.

Visit us on the Web! rhcbooks.com

Educators and librarians, for a variety of teaching tools, visit us at RHTeachersLibrarians.com

ISBN: 978-0-375-87267-9

061929.3K4/B317/A2

MANUFACTURED IN CHINA
12 11 10 9 8 7 6 5 4

Good night, laila tov

By Laurel Snyder
Illustrated by Jui Ishida

RANDOM HOUSE NEW YORK

The sun was up. The day was bright!
It filled our room with yellow light.

It woke us both, so right away . . .

We grabbed our things, were on our way.

We drove out to the oceanside.
The sand was hot. The waves were wide.

Tall grasses swayed. The salty air
Was soft and still and everywhere.

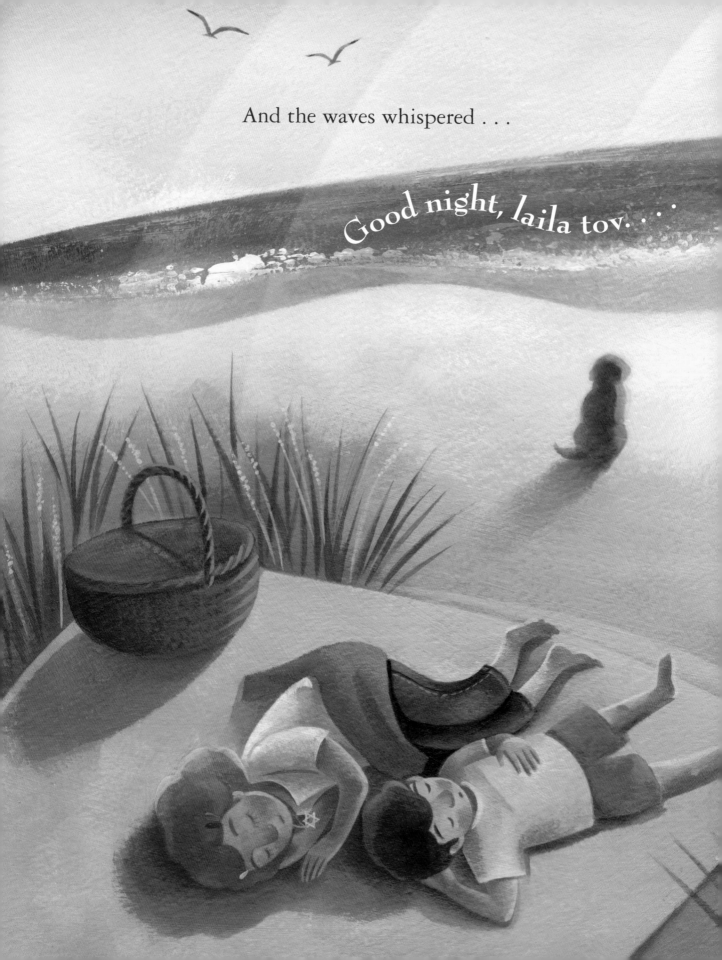

And the waves whispered . . .

Good night, laila tov. . . .

We found a place so great and green,
The deepest field we'd ever seen.

We gathered berries, sweet and red,
As shadows circled overhead.

And the sky sang . . .

Good night, laila tov. . . .

We helped our parents plant some trees.

We found some mice.

We found some bees!

Then suddenly,
The rain came down.
In plips and plops
It hit the ground.

And the storm shushed . . .

Good night, laila tov. . . .

We climbed into the sandy car
With all our treasures in a jar.

We stopped for dinner, stopped to see . . .

Stopped again so I could pee.

And the road rumbled . . .

Good night, laila tov. . . .

When we got home, the sky was black.
The cat was happy we'd come back.

And though the day was done and gone,
Somehow the lights were all still on!

Good night, laila tov. . . .